KEELEY: BOOK TWO

KEELEY'S BIG STORY

DEBORAH ELLIS

Keeley: Book Two

Keeley's Big Story

Deborah Ellis

Powell River Public Library

PENGUIN CANADA

Published by the Penguin Group

Penguin Group (Canada), 90 Eglinton Avenue East, Suite 700, Toronto, Ontario, Canada M4P 2Y3
(a division of Pearson Penguin Canada Inc.)

Penguin Group (USA) Inc., 375 Hudson Street, New York, New York 10014, U.S.A.
Penguin Books Ltd, 80 Strand, London WC2R 0RL, England
Penguin Ireland, 25 St Stephen's Green, Dublin 2, Ireland (a division of Penguin Books Ltd)
Penguin Group (Australia), 250 Camberwell Road, Camberwell, Victoria 3124, Australia
(a division of Pearson Australia Group Pty Ltd)
Penguin Books India Pvt Ltd, 11 Community Centre, Panchsheel Park, New Delhi – 110 017, India
Penguin Group (NZ), cnr Airborne and Rosedale Roads, Albany, Auckland 1310, New Zealand
(a division of Pearson New Zealand Ltd)
Penguin Books (South Africa) (Pty) Ltd, 24 Sturdee Avenue, Rosebank, Johannesburg 2196,
South Africa

Penguin Books Ltd, Registered Offices: 80 Strand, London WC2R 0RL, England

First published 2005

2 3 4 5 6 7 8 9 10 (WEB)

Copyright © Deborah Ellis, 2005
Full-page interior illustrations © Greg Banning, 2005
Chapter opening illustrations © Janet Wilson, 2005
Design: Matthews Communications Design Inc.
Map copyright © Sharon Matthews

All rights reserved. Without limiting the rights under copyright reserved above, no part of this publication may be reproduced, stored in or introduced into a retrieval system, or transmitted in any form or by any means (electronic, mechanical, photocopying, recording, or otherwise), without the prior written permission of both the copyright owner and the above publisher of this book.

Publisher's note: This book is a work of fiction. Names, characters, places, and incidents either are the product of the author's imagination or are used fictitiously, and any resemblance to actual persons living or dead, events, or locales is entirely coincidental.

Manufactured in Canada.

LIBRARY AND ARCHIVES CANADA CATALOGUING IN PUBLICATION

Ellis, Deborah, 1960–
Keeley : Keeley's big story / Deborah Ellis.

(Our Canadian girl)
"Keeley : book two".
ISBN 0-14-305010-9

I. Title. II. Title: Keeley's Big Story. III. Series.

PS8559.L5494K443 2005 jC813'.54 C2005-900216-6

Visit the Penguin Group (Canada) website at **www.penguin.ca**

To Nefisa

Yukon
Northwest Territories
Nunavut
British Columbia
Alberta
Saskatchewan
Manitoba
Ontario

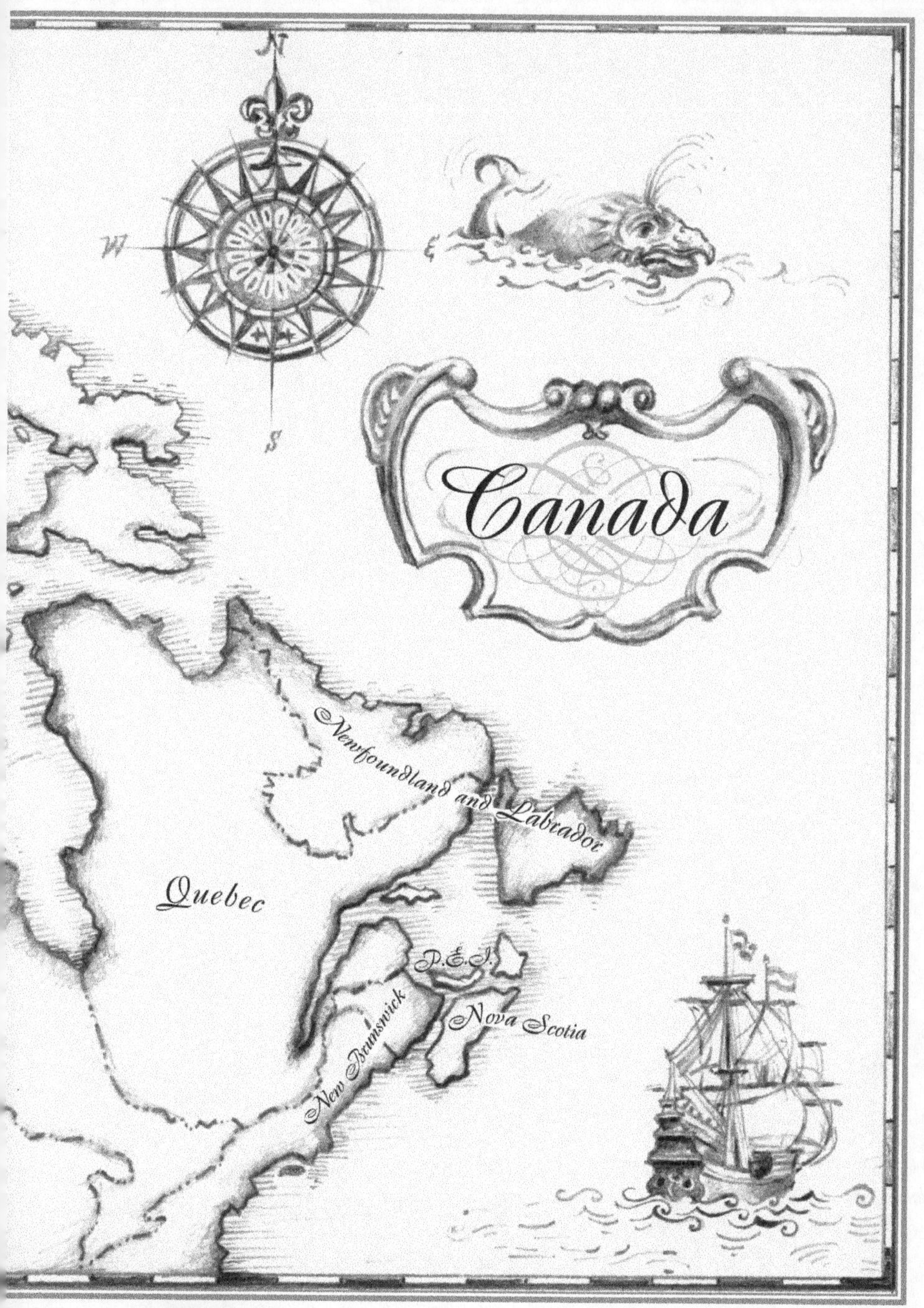

Marks the location of the story

Keeley's Story

Nine-year-old Keeley lives in the coal-mining town of Frank, in the heart of the Crowsnest Pass. She and her father, a miner, live on the top floor of a boarding house. From her window, Keeley can see Turtle Mountain—the mountain that the Kootenay Indians say will one day get up and walk.

Keeley finds Frank an interesting place to live. It's on the edge of the wilderness, with mountains, forests, and wild animals everywhere she looks. The town has attracted people from many parts of the world who have come to make their fortunes in coal.

Frank is only one coal-mining town in the Crowsnest Pass, a sixty-mile passageway through the Rocky Mountain range. Canada's hunger for coal to warm its homes and run its factories shows no signs of letting up. The town of Frank is growing so quickly that many of the new miners have to live in tents while they wait for homes to be built.

One of the things Keeley loves best about living in Frank is that there is room to run and explore and to be whatever she wants to be. She feels sorry for people who are stuck in cities, where behaviour, especially for girls, is more tightly controlled. Even though Keeley has to go to school, do chores around the boarding house, and be polite to the adults who ask tiresome questions, she still finds plenty of time to spread her wings.

At the time of this story, it is 1902 and Canada is at war, allied with the British in South Africa. But rumblings of war, and rumblings inside the mountain, have nothing to do with Keeley. Do they?

CHAPTER No 1

"Your word is chrysanthemum."

Keeley held her breath, as did the rest of the crowd in D.J. McIntyre's concert hall. The boy beside her at the centre of the stage was from Blairmore. He was the only opponent left. The spelling championship was within Keeley's reach.

The two children had beaten all the other contestants from towns along the Crowsnest Pass. This was the first annual Crowsnest Pass Spelling Bee, and Keeley was determined to win.

The Blairmore boy started slowly. "C-h-r-y-s- ..."

He put in an extra *a* instead of an *e*.

"I'm sorry, that is incorrect," the head judge said.

Keeley refrained from jumping up and down. She hadn't won yet. If she spelled her next word wrong, the Blairmore boy would get another chance at the five-dollar prize.

Time slowed for Keeley. As she waited for the head judge to give her the word that would seal her fate, she looked out over the audience. She wanted to draw luck from the people who loved her.

There was her father, of course, awake and in his Sunday best, even though he had been working in the mine all night and would have to go back to work soon. Beside him was Violet, their friend from the boarding house where they lived. Mrs. Greer, who ran the boarding house, had wanted to be there, but she was breaking in a new cook and couldn't risk leaving the kitchen.

A few rows back, Keeley's best friend, Patricia, sat between her two grandmothers, Ethel and

Mable. Even though Keeley couldn't see Patricia's hands, she knew her friend's fingers were crossed.

The town of Frank was growing, but it was still small. Keeley knew a lot of the faces in the audience, even if she didn't know their names. Of course, people from the communities of Blairmore, Hillcrest, and Belleview were also attending.

The press was there, too. Harry Matheson, the editor and sole reporter of the Frank newspaper, sat in the front row. Every now and then, Keeley saw him scribble on a notepad.

Even the judges were important people. The head judge was the district education commissioner. The other two judges were an official from the mining company that ran the Turtle Mountain coal mine and Cora Hind, the lady reporter whom Keeley had met on her first day in Frank. Miss Hind wore her usual black broad-brimmed hat, without the feathers and flowers of most women's hats.

"Spell *greedy*!" a man shouted from the audience, jumping to his feet.

"Spell *irresponsible!*" another man shouted.

"Spell *unsafe working conditions!*" a third man yelled.

Keeley was startled but not really surprised. Her father had told her that some sort of protest was being planned, although he didn't know exactly what. This was not about her, she knew. She didn't need to worry. She stood still and waited for the grown-ups to sort it out.

"Gentlemen, please resume your seats," the head judge was saying. "This is not the time or the place ..."

"We know that," one of the protesting men said, "and we apologize to the little girl. Our apologies, Miss," he said to Keeley.

Keeley smiled and nodded. She didn't mind at all. It was even a little exciting, like the times when she and Patricia stood at the window of the saloon and watched fights break out among the card players.

"We've been trying to see the mine management for weeks, but they won't see us," one of the men said. "We're taking coal out of that mountain far too quickly. It's not safe."

"The quicker the coal comes out, the quicker we can all get rich," a seated man said. "You got something against money? You one of them Communists from Russia we've been hearing about?"

"We like making money, but we want to be alive at the end of our shift, too!"

More men—and women—joined in the argument. Patricia stood up, too, and she and Keeley grinned at each other. Patricia's grandmother Ethel stared hard at the angry faces. Keeley knew that Ethel was trying to memorize the expressions so that she could carve them later into one of her crazy sculptures.

"Stop this at once!"

A voice rang out so loud and clear that it cut through the arguing. It startled Keeley so much that she jumped. The arguing immediately stopped. The hall went silent.

"Thank you," the voice said more quietly.

Keeley's eyes grew wide when she realized that the voice had come from her teacher, Miss Griffin. She'd had no idea Miss Griffin could make a noise like that.

"You may proceed," Miss Griffin said calmly to the head judge.

The head judge was quite flustered. He puffed and shuffled through his papers. Cora Hind rolled her eyes, got off her chair, and pointed to the paper on the stand in front of the head judge. She winked at Keeley and returned to her seat.

"Spell the word *sentinel,*" the head judge said.

Keeley certainly knew that one. It was the name of the local newspaper. She spelled it out in a happy shout and was dancing around the stage even before the head judge said, "That's correct," and pronounced her Spelling Champion of the Crowsnest Pass.

"And to present the award, our distinguished guest, Miss Cora Hind."

Everyone applauded. Miss Hind handed Keeley five dollars, a dictionary, and a blue ribbon with the words "Spelling Champion—1902" painted on it.

"A spelling champion, as well as a running champion," Cora Hind said, smiling.

"You remember me?" Keeley asked. On her first day in Frank, she'd won the foot race. It had been for boys only, but Keeley had entered it because there hadn't been a race for girls. Cora Hind had been there, and she had made the judge, a government minister from Ottawa, give Keeley the medal, even though he hadn't wanted to award it to a girl.

"Of course I remember you. I expect great things from you. Don't let me down."

"I won't," Keeley promised, shaking Cora Hind's hand. She then had to pose for a photo with her teacher and with the other spellers before she could leave the stage and join the after-bee party.

Patricia was waiting for her. "I knew you'd win," she exclaimed as she pulled Keeley toward the refreshment table.

Pop and Violet found Keeley there. He twirled Keeley in a big hug, almost knocking over a tray of apple cider. "I'm so happy for you," he said. "I'm happy for me, too. No more do I have to listen to you practise your spelling."

"Oh, it hasn't been so bad," Violet said. As usual, Violet looked and smelled like a frilly flower. "My spelling has certainly improved from helping you, and I'm sure your father's has, too."

"It has," Pop admitted, "but I'm still glad it's over. I've started spelling out loud in the mine—c-o-a-l, a-x-e. The other miners laugh at me."

"They're just jealous."

One of the miners who had protested came up to them. "Your little girl certainly kept her cool up there when the shouting started."

"Keeley doesn't rattle easily," Pop said proudly.

"As long as she stays out of the mines. I was one of the men who dug you out that night," he said, nodding to Keeley. "Don't worry that you don't recognize me. I was covered in coal dust then."

Soon after moving to Frank, Keeley was dared to spend a night in the mine. She had been trapped there for a while, when rock from the mountain shaking had fallen into the tunnel.

"I stay out of the mine now," Keeley said.

The miner smiled and then turned to Keeley's father. "I don't know if our protest did any good."

"It will certainly get people talking," Pop said.

"Well, that's a start." The miner bid them good afternoon. Pop and Violet saw some other people across the hall they wanted to talk to.

"Are you going to hog all the cookies?" Peter, one of Keeley's classmates and the boy who had dared her to spend the night in the mine, reached between Patricia and Keeley to get to the cookies.

"You didn't last long up there," Patricia said. Peter had been one of the spellers, but he had been taken out early.

"Who cares about spelling?" Peter replied.

Keeley waved her five dollars at him.

Patricia turned her back to him. "We have more important things to talk about. Mrs. Johnston had one of her husband's shirts stolen right off her laundry line."

"I can still hear you," Peter said, his mouth full of cookie. "And it wasn't a shirt. It was a pair of trousers."

"It was a shirt," Patricia said, turning back around. "The mystery thief has struck again."

"Did Mrs. Johnston see anything?" Keeley asked.

"No. She put three shirts on the line to dry, and when she went out to take them down, she was missing a shirt."

"She was missing trousers," Peter said.

"We're ignoring you," Keeley said to him. "You don't know what you're taking about, and you're not brave enough to do anything about it anyway." She turned to Patricia. "Mrs. Greer is missing an axe from the wood pile and some dishes, too. The thief came right into her kitchen!"

"Someone—I forget who—said they were missing a chicken," Patricia said. "And I heard

Mrs. Nesbit say that someone stole one of her pies right off the windowsill where it was cooling."

"I'm braver than you," Peter said, butting into the conversation. "I hear the thief is a wild man who comes down from the mountains. He's half-man, half-bear."

"Well, if you're so brave, why don't you catch him, then?"

"I think I'll just go and do that," Peter said, grabbing more cookies before swaggering away.

Keeley glowered at him as she watched him go.

"Forget about him," Patricia said. "What are you going to spend your five dollars on?"

That was a much more pleasant topic, even though Keeley was sure that her father would make her put it all in the bank. She and Patricia discussed it over cider and cookies until it was time to go home.

CHAPTER No 2

"I've got it! I've got it!" Keeley ran into Patricia's yard, waving a copy of the Frank *Sentinel* in one hand and clutching a bag of penny candy in the other.

Patricia's Granny Ethel was in the yard, using her axe to shape a stump into one of her sculptures. Keeley was too excited to stop and admire it. She waved the newspaper in greeting and kept running.

Behind the house, Keeley stopped at the foot of the biggest tree. "Let me up! I've got it!"

Patricia's face appeared through the leaves. "What's the password?"

"Oh, for goodness' sake, not now. I've got the newspaper, the one with the spelling bee article in it."

Patricia tossed the rope ladder down so fast that it almost hit Keeley in the head. Keeley scrambled up into the tree house.

Patricia's two grandmothers had built her the tree house. Her Granny Ethel had carved into it the faces of people in Patricia's life, for decoration. It was a secure place, safe from boys who Patricia and Keeley didn't like and hidden from the prying eyes of adults—although Patricia's grannies were not the prying type.

"Did you read it yet?" Patricia asked, accepting the bag of candy that Keeley held out to her. Keeley's father had, as expected, made her put her prize money in the bank, but he had given her ten cents to spend on candy. That was enough for several weeks' worth of licorice, caramels, and barley sugar.

"Of course I didn't read it. I wouldn't read it without you—hey, is that my face?"

Keeley stepped over to the wall for a closer look. It *was* her face carved into the board. It even had her braids.

"Granny Ethel carved it early this morning. She tried to tell me the fairies did it. But you can look at your face later. Let's read the article."

Keeley sat on the floor beside her friend, spread out the newspaper, and dipped her hand into the paper bag for a caramel.

"You're on page one!"

"Where else would I be?" Keeley replied. The photo at the top of the article was of her and Miss Griffin.

"You look good," Patricia declared. "Miss Griffin looks stiff."

"Miss Griffin *is* stiff," Keeley said, "but she sure can bellow." She started to read the article out loud. "'Local student Keeley O'Brien beat out many others from the region to win the title of Spelling Champion of the Crowsnest Pass.' There are three spelling mistakes in that sentence alone."

"Who cares? Keep reading."

"I care! It's an article about good spelling. Everything in it should be spelled properly."

"Keep reading."

"You read it," Keeley said. "If I listen, I won't see the mistakes."

Patricia read the rest of the article out loud. "It mentions your name three times," she said. "Peter isn't mentioned at all."

That made Keeley feel better. "He was awful at the party, bragging that he could capture that thief. If I wasn't forbidden from daring, I would have dared him to do it just so I could see him fail."

"Why don't we capture the thief?" Patricia suggested. "I'd like to be in the newspaper, too, and I'll certainly never win a spelling bee."

Keeley's eyes lit up. "We'd be big heroes! What should we do first?"

"Gather information, I think."

"Like reporters," Keeley said. "Cora Hind told me that she expects big things from me. This will be a big thing."

The snack-time bell rang. Patricia pulled on the rope that stretched from the tree house to the main house. A basket with a bottle of milk and warm doughnuts, glazed with honey from Granny Mable's bees, came into the tree house. Keeley put the candy into their emergency rations tin to be saved for a day without doughnuts.

The girls ate their snack and planned what to do.

"We should watch out for anything suspicious," Keeley said, "and report to each other every day." She noticed a book that was lying face down on the tree house floor. "What are you reading now?"

"The Arabian Nights." Patricia licked honey from her fingers.

Keeley picked up the newspaper again. "I still don't like all these spelling mistakes. When we capture the thief and become big heroes, I don't want that article to be full of mistakes like this one is."

"Why don't you go tell the newspaper man to start working on his spelling?" Patricia said, taking her book into her lap.

"That's a good idea," Keeley said, standing up. "Are you coming with me?"

But Patricia was already back with Ali Baba, so Keeley headed down the ladder on her own, taking the newspaper with her.

She waved goodbye to Granny Ethel, but Ethel was too engrossed in her sculpture to really notice.

They are a strange family, Keeley thought as she headed down the trail, *but I sure do like them.*

The trail into the main part of town wound along the Oldman River. Keeley saw a small herd of deer, with their new fawns, prance away from her into a thicket. She waved to Andy Grissick, the old trapper. He was standing by his tent, where he slept winter and summer.

"Keeley," he called out, "have you seen my frying pan?"

"No, I haven't," she called back, but she didn't stop to talk to him. He was a wonderful story-teller, and she knew from experience that once she started listening to him, it would be very hard to pull herself away.

"Are you sure you kids haven't been playing games again?" he asked.

After that, of course, she had to stop and help him look.

"I've had that frying pan for years," he grumbled. "I had it when I went looking for the Lost Lemon Mine. Did I ever tell you that story?"

They searched the campsite and the bushes around it, but the frying pan wasn't there. "I'll keep my eyes open for it," Keeley promised as she went on her way. She hated to see Mr. Grissick look so sad.

The town of Frank was only officially seven months old, but it was growing fast. Keeley had been there since September 10, which was both the day the town was founded and her birthday. It was now May. It seemed to Keeley that every time she went outside Mrs. Greer's boarding house, there were new people and new things to see in the town.

Keeley passed the new miners' tents, clumped together almost like their own village. There weren't enough real houses built in the town yet, and not all the miners could afford to pay for rooms in a lodging house. Some of the miners had their children and wives with them, who were cooking or doing laundry over outdoor fires.

Dominion Street, the main street of Frank, was full of people doing their Saturday afternoon shopping or enjoying a bit of free time between the workweek and the stuffy formality of Sunday. The broad sidewalks were dotted with window shoppers and small groups of people in conversation. Keeley passed the tavern but did not stop to look in the window to see whether any gamblers were fighting, the way she usually did when she was with Patricia. Today, she had a mission.

The Frank *Sentinel* had a small office on the main street, across from the photographer's studio. Keeley went inside. Harry Matheson was at the counter, helping the town's undertaker to word an advertisement.

Keeley waited with extreme patience for about

fifteen seconds, then blurted out, "Why do you need to advertise?"

The two men frowned at her, annoyed at the interruption.

"Everybody knows who you are and where you are," Keeley continued. Too often, once her mouth started talking, it kept on talking whether anyone wanted to hear her or not. "You're the only undertaker in Frank. Where else would dead people go?"

The undertaker's expression froze for a moment, and he looked from Keeley to Mr. Matheson and then back to Keeley. "You're right," he said. "I don't need to advertise." He put on his tall, black hat and said to Mr. Matheson, "I'll bid good day to you, sir." He left the newspaper office.

Keeley watched him go and then put the newspaper on the counter, ready to state her business.

"You just cost me a customer," Mr. Matheson said.

"But he really didn't need to advertise."

"This paper depends on money from advertisements," Mr. Matheson said. "You have just cost me money. Keep that in mind the next time you burst in on someone's conversation."

"I'm sorry," Keeley said.

"You've been telling me for six months that you want to be a reporter like Cora Hind. Do you think she would be foolish enough to cost her newspaper money?"

"I said I was sorry." Keeley hated it when adults went on and on about the same point.

"All right, then. Now, what brings you here?"

"This article." Keeley pointed to the newspaper. "It's full of spelling mistakes."

"Oh. Is that all?"

"Is that all? Isn't spelling important?"

"Are all the facts correct?"

"Well, yes," Keeley admitted.

"The facts are the most important part," Mr. Matheson said. "Perfect spelling would be nice, but I was never any good at it."

"I'm good at it," Keeley said. She had a sudden brilliant idea. "You should give me a job! I could check your newspaper for spelling mistakes!"

"Your father doesn't approve of children working," Mr. Matheson said. "He and I have had one or two conversations on the matter over an evening whiskey."

"Maybe if I ask him?"

"Let me think about it. If I decide it's a good idea, I'll talk to him."

"Will you decide soon?" Keeley asked. Mr. Matheson frowned at her. "All right, I'm going," she said.

"Goodbye," Mr. Matheson said, "and don't cost me any more customers!"

CHAPTER No. 3

"Ouch! You're pulling all my hair o—!"

The last word of Keeley's complaint was lost when Lillian Clark, Mrs. Greer's helper, poured cold water over Keeley's head.

"How you do carry on over a bit of hair washing," Lillian said, squeezing the suds out of Keeley's hair.

"Mrs. Greer is more gentle. And she heats the water!"

"Well, Mrs. Greer is busy. Stop complaining. It's a fine, warm day. A little cold water is good for you."

Keeley was bent over a tub in the boarding house yard. She opened her mouth to complain again but got another taste of cold water. She closed her mouth and kept it closed until Lillian declared her done.

"Now, you can return the favour by using all this water to water the vegetable garden. And be gentle, mind you. Don't drown the new plants." She tossed a towel over Keeley's head.

"What about my comb out?" Keeley called from underneath the towel.

"Can't you do anything for yourself?" Lillian called back on her way into the boarding house.

"I can't wait to be old like she is," Keeley grumbled, rubbing the towel over her hair. "I'm going to be mean to everybody and get away with it."

Keeley tried pulling a comb through her thick, dark hair, but it kept getting stuck. *It will be easier when it dries,* she decided as she hung the towel on the line to dry.

She thought about throwing the washing water out, just to spite Lillian, but then Mrs. Greer would hear about it, and then her father, and it just seemed like too much trouble. She hauled the first bucket of water from the tub over to the vegetable patch and began watering carefully. She used an old tin cup that hung in the garden to put water at the base of each new plant, so the roots could drink it up.

She heard people murmuring in the yard next door. She listened, but she couldn't understand what they were saying. *Why would people murmur?* she wondered. Because they have a secret, was the answer she came up with. What sort of a secret? Maybe about the thief! She had to hear more.

Keeley filled another bucket and took it over to the plants closest to the bushes. She could hear a little better, but the words still weren't clear.

The plants could wait. Keeley crawled into the bushes as quietly as she could. A good reporter had to go to any length to get her story.

The bushes were thick and low to the ground. Some had thorns that stuck in Keeley's clothes and hair. She yanked herself free, squirming closer to the neighbour's yard. The voices were getting clearer. She headed for a patch of daylight.

"Ohhph!" A branch of some sort had her in its grip. She tried to pull herself forward, but she heard the sound of cloth ripping on her back.

I'd better back up, she thought. Mrs. Greer, who kept her clothes mended, would be unhappy if she came home with yet another big tear.

Keeley tried to back up, but another branch lodged its hooks in her wet hair. She tried to pull her head free, but it hurt too much.

She raised an arm to try to untangle her hair, but her sleeve got caught on something, too!

Keeley balanced on two knees and one hand, with her head caught, her arm caught, and her dress caught.

Now what do I do? she wondered.

The voices went quiet. From her strange position, Keeley saw several pairs of feet come into the little patch of daylight she'd been heading for. She kept very still, hoping they would go away without noticing her.

The bushes were thick and low to the ground.... She yanked herself free, squirming closer to the neighbour's yard.

"Are you looking for something?"

Keeley recognized the voice of her neighbour, Mrs. Livingston. She had to reply. "I'm watering the vegetable plants," she said.

"Need any help?" another woman asked. Keeley didn't recognize that voice.

"No, no, I think I can manage. Thank you very much, though." *Go away,* Keeley pleaded silently.

Just when she thought it couldn't get any worse, Keeley heard a third voice. It was the worst voice in the world she could hear at this moment. It was Peter's.

"Where's your watering can?" he asked. Then he burst into laughter.

Keeley couldn't see their faces, but she knew from the way the women were talking that they were trying hard not to laugh, as well. "You seem to be in a bit of a tangle there, dear. Let us help you out."

Hands reached through the bushes and tugged at her hair and her clothes. Peter kept laughing while he helped untangle her hair.

"If you were trying to hide, you were doing a poor job of it," he said. "Your back end was sticking up. It was almost as high as Turtle Mountain!"

"Don't say 'back end' to me, Peter Johnson," Keeley said. "That's terrible language to use to a lady."

On the word *lady,* Keeley was yanked free, right into the neighbour's yard. Her hair was wild, her dress was torn, and she was covered in dirt and leaves.

The two women joined Peter and burst out laughing. Keeley flung back her messy hair, thrust her nose into the air, and got out of the yard as quickly as possible.

She ran into the boarding house yard, hoping to get up to the attic room she shared with her father without anybody seeing her. No such luck. She ran straight into Violet, who was coming out of the front door, her painting supplies in her hands.

"My goodness, Keeley—what happened to you?"

If anyone but Violet—and her Pop—had spoken to her at that moment, Keeley would have yelled at them, she was so upset. But it was impossible to yell at Violet.

"I made an idiot of myself," she said, "and in front of Peter!"

"I know just the cure for that," Violet said. "Come with me." She held the door open for Keeley to go inside.

"But you were going painting."

"I was going to paint the mountain," Violet said. "It will still be there later. Mountains don't just get up and move."

They went upstairs to Violet's room. It was a lovely, sunny room, all lacy and pretty like Violet. It had a table where Violet would serve refreshments to all the gentlemen friends who came to see her.

"We'll have you fixed up in no time," Violet said. Using her lotions and brushes, she soon had Keeley cleaned up and her hair smoothed out. "Take off that dress and I'll mend it for you," she said when she had tied Keeley's braids. "Mrs. Greer will never know unless she looks closely—I'm not as good a stitcher as she is—and she is far too busy to look closely."

Keeley sat on the end of Violet's bed and watched her sew. "How am I going to face Peter?"

"Well, suppose you tell me what you were doing in the bushes."

"I heard voices in the next yard, but I couldn't really tell what they were saying. I was trying to get close enough to hear, but I didn't want to be seen. I was … I was training to be a reporter." She was going to say *pretending,* but that sounded too childish.

Violet put down the mending and put her arm around Keeley. "The next time you see Peter, no matter how much he teases you, just keep saying to yourself, 'I'm going to be a reporter. I'm going to be a reporter.' That will help you remember that you've got hopes and dreams. You have them on days when everything goes right and on days when you behave like an idiot."

Keeley felt a thousand times better when she left Violet's room. She even remembered to finish watering the vegetable garden. At least there was something Lillian couldn't complain about.

"Speeches, speeches, speeches, all grown-ups do is make speeches," Keeley muttered, shuffling her feet as much as she dared. She knew that wasn't true—she knew plenty of adults who did other things. Her father wrote poetry. Violet painted pictures. Granny Mable took care of bees, and so on. But Empire Day brought out all the speechmakers.

"Begun in 1897 by Mrs. Clementina Fessenden of Hamilton, Ontario, Empire Day allows us to celebrate the birth of Queen Victoria and to show our joy at being loyal subjects of the British

Empire," the mayor of Frank droned on.

Keeley looked at the banners that some of the townspeople carried: Sons of Canada, Sons of England, Sons of Scotland. She'd seen a Votes for Women banner at the start of the ceremony, but the constable had made the women put it away.

Other groups of people didn't have banners. Keeley guessed they were from other countries. There were people in Frank from Sweden, Poland, Italy—lots of places. Keeley thought they should hold up banners, too.

"Hey—what are we?" She nudged Patricia. "Are we Canadian or are we British?"

"You're idiots," Peter said. He was standing in the row behind them.

Keeley, using excellent aim, brought her heel down on Peter's toes. In the next instant, she found herself being pulled away from the other children and made to stand beside Miss Griffin.

A lady wearing a big, ugly hat made the next speech, urging people to contribute to the war charities.

"Those of us who cannot fight on the front line of the British Campaign in Africa can show our support for the Empire by giving money to the Fund for Disabled Soldiers, the Soldiers of the Queen Relief Fund, or the Absent-Minded Beggars Fund."

Keeley wondered if she should take her five-dollar prize money out of the bank and give it to the soldiers. Plus, she still had five cents of the money her father had given her. Then the moment of generous feeling passed, and Keeley was glad—she wanted to spend her five cents on candy.

The lady stepped off the stage, and Keeley's hopes rose. Maybe that was the last of the speeches, and Keeley and her classmates could march back to school where, she was sure, it was recess time.

But no. The mayor got up again.

"And now, let's show our appreciation for some of the fighting men from the Crowsnest Pass."

It was fun to cheer and make noise with the rest of the crowd as a row of men in military uniform got up on the platform. One had a bandage over his left eye. Another was on crutches and had only one leg. Many had shiny medals on their chests. Keeley noticed that these men didn't cheer.

The crowd sang "The Maple Leaf Forever," and then bowed their heads while a minister prayed for God to watch over the British Empire. Finally, after singing "God Save The King," the ceremony was over.

"Line up, everyone," Miss Griffin said to the class. "We will return to the school in an orderly fashion." Keeley started to join Patricia, but Miss Griffin's hand came down on her shoulder. There was no escape. Miss Griffin looked prim and proper, but her fingers had a grip like an eagle's talons.

They waited for the crowd to clear out enough to be able to walk through it in a way Miss Griffin considered orderly. Patricia sent Keeley a sympathetic look. Peter stuck out his tongue at her.

"Peter, since your tongue needs fresh air, you may spend the entire recess period standing on the school steps with your tongue out," Miss Griffin declared.

Keeley tried to look triumphant without changing the expression on her face, in case Miss Griffin was watching. It was difficult to do. Fortunately, a fight broke out between two boys farther up the line. Miss Griffin went to separate them, leaving Keeley alone.

One of the young uniformed men from the stage slowly moved by on his crutches. The lower part of one of his pant legs was folded neatly and held against his thigh with a pin. He stopped near Keeley to catch his breath.

"Where's your leg?" Keeley asked before realizing it might be a rude question.

"In Africa," the young man replied.

Keeley looked down at her own legs and wondered what it would be like to have a part of herself so far away. "Do you miss it?" she asked.

"What do you think?"

Miss Griffin came back. "All right, Keeley. Let's join the others."

"Miss Griffin, this man left his leg in Africa."

Miss Griffin shook the soldier's hand. They were introducing themselves when an army officer walked over to them. Keeley could tell that he was more important than the soldier, because his uniform was fancier.

"Shouldn't you be with your unit?" the officer asked the soldier. Without waiting for a reply, he tipped his hat at Miss Griffin and extended his hand.

"Good afternoon, Miss Griffin," he said. "There has been no news yet, I'm afraid."

"Thank you for telling me," Miss Griffin said.

"You will be sure to inform us if you hear anything?" the officer asked.

"You have already made that request," replied Miss Griffin. "You will excuse me. I have to get these children back to school."

Miss Griffin put her arm on Keeley's shoulder to turn her around.

"If he can still run, he should keep on running," the soldier said.

"What was that, Private?" the captain snapped.

"Nothing, Captain," the soldier said.

Keeley laughed. The word *captain* had come out sounding like one of the curse words the drunks used when they were being thrown out of the bar.

The class marched back to school. Keeley spent the recess writing "I will behave myself at ceremonies" one hundred times on the chalkboard. Miss Griffin did not tell her who the officer was, and Keeley did not get to see Peter standing with his tongue sticking out.

CHAPTER No 5

Keeley stared at the rows and rows of tiny metal blocks on the rack in front of her. Each block had a raised letter on it.

"These are the rows of type," Mr. Matheson said to her. She was at the newspaper office for her first morning of work. Her father had agreed to let her help Mr. Matheson. "I take the letters and put them into this tray, spelling out the words I want."

Keeley looked closer. The letters were backwards. Mr. Matheson read her thoughts.

"They'll come out in the right direction when they're printed onto paper," he said.

"It must take you forever to print an article," Keeley said.

"You get faster with practice." Mr. Matheson put paper cones over his lower shirtsleeves.

"Why do you wear those?"

"To keep the ink off my shirt."

"Can I wear some?"

"I think I'll keep you safely away from the ink." He pointed to a high stool at the counter where he wanted her to sit. "When I finish setting the type on an article, I'll print one page, and you can check it over for spelling mistakes."

"Can I write an article?" she asked. "I know a great news story. It's all about the mysterious disappearance of things."

"What things?"

"Mr. Johnston's shirt, and Mrs. Nesbit's pie, and ..."

"Sounds like the crime of the century. You've solved this mystery, have you?"

"Well, no," Keeley admitted, "but I'm going to."

"When you do, maybe we'll put it in the newspaper. Until then, your job is spelling." He pointed to a few pages he had printed out before Keeley arrived.

Keeley sat down on the stool, her legs dangling, and got to work. The first article was about the prime minister's speech to the House of Commons. It wasn't very interesting.

"How does somebody get to be prime minister?" she asked.

"I don't think you can ask questions and check spelling at the same time."

Keeley frowned and turned her attention back to the prime minister. She found three spelling mistakes, circled them, and wrote out the proper spelling in the margin beside each one.

"Here's a word you got wrong, but I don't know what the right word is," she said.

"What word?"

Keeley squinted at it. "I don't even know how to say it."

"Read out the letters."

She spelled it out. "B-o-e-r."

The editor thought a moment. "I'm sure that's right." He picked up another newspaper, the *Calgary Herald,* and showed Keeley the headline. "Yes, B-o-e-r."

Keeley read the headline. "What does it mean?"

"There's a war going on in South Africa now against the Boers. That's the name of some of the people who live there. Canadians are fighting in it."

"I met a soldier who lost his leg in Africa. It's so far away to have people angry with us. Why are we there?"

"Because England told us to be there."

"But why?"

"I don't think you can ask questions and check spelling at the same time," Mr. Matheson said again. His thick blond hair was streaked with ink from pushing his hair back off his face.

Keeley slowly read over the article about the Boer War, making sure that all the letters were the right ones and that they were all in the right places. By the time she reached the end of the article, she understood that some Canadians had died, but she didn't understand any more than that.

Keeley had a habit of tugging on one of her braids when she was concentrating. Halfway through an article on the rush for land in Saskatchewan, she realized she was holding an untied ribbon, and her long brown hair was hanging down in her face.

"Oh, bother." She was no good at braiding, even worse at it than her father was. Violet usually did her hair for her in the mornings, but Violet wasn't around. She took a quick look at Mr. Matheson. He didn't look like someone who spent a lot of time braiding.

Keeley held the ribbon in her hand and wondered what to do. Since she couldn't rebraid her hair, she tied it in a ponytail and then unbraided the other side so it would look the same. As she was reaching up to retie her ribbon, a very curious sight caught her eye through the window.

Miss Griffin was hurrying along the sidewalk on the other side of the street. That wasn't unusual in itself. Lots of people were on the sidewalks doing their Saturday shopping. But Miss Griffin wasn't shopping. She was fluttering along in a most unteacherlike way!

Her coat wasn't buttoned properly, her hat was askew, and her arms were full of loosely wrapped brown paper bundles. Keeley knew that Miss Griffin knew how to tie a bundle properly. She'd taught a lesson on it just two weeks ago.

Where could her teacher be going in such a state? It was Saturday, so she wasn't late for school or church.

One of the bundles slipped out of Miss Griffin's arms and fell onto the sidewalk. Miss Griffin stopped, but before she could bend down to retrieve it herself, a man came by, weaving along the sidewalk as if he'd been celebrating Saturday night a little early. He bumped into Miss Griffin, tried to give her a dignified tip of the cap, and bent down to get her bundle for her. He picked it up, tearing it open in the process.

Keeley's eyes grew wide as a large, white man's shirt fluttered from the end of his arm like a flag. Miss Griffin snatched it away from him, tucked it under her arm, and hurried down the street. She had to push her way through the people crowding the sidewalk.

Keeley felt a flash of pity for her teacher as she watched Miss Griffin bump into two older ladies in her hurry to get away. Where was she going in such a hurry, and why was she carrying a man's shirt? Keeley leaned over the counter, watching her teacher go. Miss Griffin moved so quickly. Keeley stood on the rung of her stool, leaning farther over, trying to see where Miss Griffin was going in such a hurry. She had to balance on one leg and two arms, then one leg and one arm, and then—

The stool slipped out from underneath her. Keeley waved her arms, trying to keep upright, and for a long, terrible moment, she felt almost suspended in the air. Then the moment ended, and she was flying, crashing into Mr. Matheson. She put out her hands to break her fall, latched onto the trays of small letters, and brought the whole thing crashing down on her and Mr. Matheson.

For a moment, neither of them moved. Keeley heard the sounds of the tiny metal letters hitting the floor all around them, like hail hitting a roof.

Maybe I'm dead, Keeley thought. Maybe Mr. Matheson was dead. If either of those things were true, maybe she could avoid punishment.

But Mr. Matheson was very much alive, and so was she. The wooden trays that had held the type were heavy on her. Mr. Matheson pushed them away.

"Are you all right?" he asked, sounding more concerned than angry, although Keeley was pretty sure that anger was about to arrive.

Before she could answer, she heard the bell ring over the newspaper office door. She looked up. It was her father.

"I see Keeley is being a big help to you," he said, kneeling beside her. "Are you hurt?"

She put out her hands to break her fall, latched onto the trays of small letters, and brought the whole thing crashing down on her and Mr. Matheson.

"I'm all right," she said. "I made a big mess, though."

"I'll go fetch some more hands."

He was back in a remarkably short time, accompanied by Patricia and her grandmothers.

"It's lucky that this happened on a Saturday," Keeley said. "If it had been during the week, Mable and Ethel wouldn't have been downtown, and Patricia and I would have been at school. We wouldn't have been able to help."

It wasn't until her enthusiasm was met by Mr. Matheson's glower that Keeley realized what a foolish thing she'd said. Patricia gave Keeley a sympathetic smile but wisely stayed silent.

If Mr. Matheson had been left to clean up the mess with only Keeley to help, he may well have fired her there and then. But he quickly got into a deep discussion with her father, Mable, and Ethel. Keeley didn't understand it all, but she recognized the words *poetry, journalism,* and *revolution*. Ethel and Mr. Matheson both knew a lot about the history of the alphabet and had a good-natured argument about how the letter *h* was first formed. Patricia seemed to be more interested in the grown-ups' conversation than in her friend today, which annoyed Keeley to no end. She had wanted to tell Patricia what she had seen! She sighed deeply and continued to clean up the letters.

"Join us for supper," her father invited Mr. Matheson when all the little letters were back where they should be.

"I still have a newspaper to put out," Mr. Matheson said.

"I guess I wasn't much help to you today," Keeley said. "I'm awfully sorry."

"Next Saturday will be better," he said. "How did it happen, anyway?"

Keeley was suddenly the centre of attention. "I was looking at something out the window," she said, feeling foolish.

"Next time, have her sit with her back to the street," her father suggested. The adults shook hands, Mable promised to drop off some of the honey-wine she was famous for, and they all left the newspaper office. Patricia and her grandmothers went off to finish their shopping.

Keeley's father treated her to supper at the Palm Restaurant, then they walked back to the boarding house. It was a beautiful evening, with the scents of spring filling the air.

"We should climb all of these mountains," Keeley said, "one after the other."

"There are more mountains beyond these," her father said. "We could keep climbing and climbing, up and down, all the way to the top of Canada, then turn around and go all the way down to South America."

Keeley stopped walking. Coming down the path through the trees was Miss Griffin.

She was walking more slowly this time, her eyes downcast. The bundles she carried now were different. One was small and tucked up in a roll of brown paper. A shawl was wrapped around the other. This bundle was shaped like a … a frying pan?

"Good evening, Miss Griffin," Keeley said as the teacher got closer. Miss Griffin kept walking.

Keeley's father tipped his hat. "A very pleasant evening, isn't it, Miss Griffin?"

Miss Griffin seemed startled that someone was talking to her. She said "Good evening," in reply, but absent-mindedly, and kept on walking.

Keeley stared after her until her father gently pulled her along.

"That's very strange," Keeley said. "She ran through the town earlier, her arms full of bundles, then she comes out of the forest with only one bundle. I wonder what's going on?"

"Don't go poking about in people's lives," her father said. "Folks are entitled to their secrets."

Secrets, Keeley thought. She wondered just what sort of secrets her teacher was keeping.

"Harvey's shirt reappeared on the wash line this morning," Keeley heard Mrs. Johnston say. Keeley and her father were standing outside the church after Sunday services. She wanted her dinner—it had been a long service—but grown-ups liked to stand around and talk and talk and talk. Mrs. Johnston was talking to someone Keeley couldn't see through the crowd. Even though she couldn't see, Keeley saw no reason she shouldn't eavesdrop. A good reporter was always on the job. She leaned back a bit to get her ears closer to the conversation.

"There it was, hanging on the wash line, as though it had been there all along."

"That shirt probably just blew away in the wind," Mrs. Johnston's companion said. "Somebody recognized it and put it back on your wash line as a good deed. No mystery there. Now, if my pie were to reappear …"

Keeley leaned way back and would have fallen if her father hadn't put his hand out to catch her.

"Keeley, you were asked a question."

Mr. Swanson, a friend of her father's from the mine, was looking down at her with a patient smile on his face. His handlebar moustache stuck out so far from his face that Keeley was sure a bird would land on it.

"I was asking if you're looking forward to the summer holidays."

With her father watching, Keeley was careful not to let her annoyance show. She gave the expected answer to Mr. Swanson's silly question, wondering why adults always seemed to interrupt the good moments.

Mrs. Greer's Sunday dinner at the boarding house was a large, heavy affair, with a roast, potatoes, and pie. Keeley's stomach felt ready to burst by the time the meal was over and she was allowed to leave. She started running toward Patricia's house but had to slow down. She was too full of dinner to run.

Patricia was in the yard, playing croquet with her grandmothers. At least, at first glance, Keeley thought it was croquet. The mallets were there, and the balls and the wickets, but there seemed to be a lot more involved than in the ordinary croquet game.

"You hit your ball without asking for a rhyming word," Ethel accused Mable. "Run around the frog three times."

Mable, holding her mallet over her head, ran around the wooden statue that looked very little like a frog to Keeley. "There are too many rules," Mable called out as she ran.

"There's not too many if you pay attention," Patricia said. "And because you complained, you have to rhyme two words instead of just one—robin and pocket."

Mable rhymed pocket with locket, but got stuck on robin.

"Keeley, come and join us," Ethel invited.

"I don't know how to play."

"Neither do we," Patricia said. "It's a Mad Croquet Game, you know, like the Mad Hatter's Tea Party."

"What are you talking about?" Keeley asked, picking up a mallet and looking for a ball to hit.

"It's from *Alice in Wonderland,*" Mable said.

"You really should read more books," Patricia told her. "In Mad Croquet, we make up the rules as we go along, and you have to give a reason for the rule."

"All madness contains the kernel of sanity," Mable said.

"She means all nonsense contains a seed of sense," Ethel translated.

Keeley still didn't know what they were talking about, but she jumped into the game. No one kept score, so there were no winners or losers, and the game ended when Ethel decided she needed a cup of tea. She and Mable went into the house. Patricia and Keeley climbed into the tree house.

"Miss Griffin is up to something," Keeley said as her friend pulled up the trap door.

"You mean something besides making your life miserable?"

"Much besides that." Keeley told her what she'd seen Saturday and what she'd heard after church.

"The Strange Case of the Reappearing Shirt," Patricia said. "We need Sherlock Holmes."

"Who?"

"You really should read more books."

"I think we should keep a close watch on Miss Griffin. I think she's the thief. I think she's been stealing things around town and has a treasure cave somewhere where she hides everything."

"I thought the thief was a wild man who lived on the mountain," Patricia said. "Wait! Maybe

Miss Griffin turns into a werewolf at the full moon. She becomes half-wolf, half-teacher." Then Patricia had a more sensible thought. "If she's the thief, why would she return the shirt?"

"Maybe she feels bad about stealing because of the Commandments, but she can't help herself," Keeley suggested.

Patricia chewed on the end of one of her braids. "So, we'd actually be helping her if we discovered her secret and made her stop. Just like the wolf-man who really wanted to be put out of his misery with a silver bullet."

"No bullets!" Keeley was appalled. "I really don't know what you're talking about half the time."

Patricia waved away Keeley's reaction. She didn't want to interrupt their discussion with an explanation of yet another story her friend hadn't read. "All I'm saying is that Miss Griffin probably *wants* to stop taking things but can't, so if *we* stop her, we'd be doing her a favour."

"Exactly." Keeley liked the sound of that.

"There's just one problem," Patricia said. "My grandmothers don't like me sticking my nose into other people's business. They say too many people have tried to tell them how to run their lives, and it's bad manners."

"My father doesn't like me poking my nose in either," Keeley said. It was a problem.

"Still, if it's for Miss Griffin's own good …," Patricia suggested.

"And the good of the whole town, if we stop things from disappearing …," Keeley continued.

"The whole town would be grateful to us," Patricia said.

"Especially when they read my story about our bravery in the newspaper." That was the deciding point for Keeley. "I'm prepared to get into trouble if it means we can help so many people."

"So am I," Patricia agreed.

Feeling very noble and self-sacrificing, the two friends began making plans for keeping an eye on Miss Griffin.

CHAPTER No. 7

Keeley and Patricia kept a close eye on Miss Griffin all through the next week. They checked in with each other after school every day. Their teacher didn't do any more mad dashes through town, at least not when they were around, but she didn't act normally either.

"She's letting the boys get away with everything," Patricia said.

"She's letting *me* get away with everything," Keeley said. "I haven't done my arithmetic homework all week, and she hasn't said a thing."

"Her mind is on her crimes." Patricia pushed

her glasses higher on her nose and folded her arms across her chest. "There isn't enough time during the week for her to get to her treasure. We'll follow her this weekend."

They didn't get a chance to do this until midway through Saturday afternoon. They both had chores to do, and Keeley also had her job at the newspaper. The first place they checked after they met was Andy Grissick's camp by the Oldman River. Andy was dozing by the riverbank, his fishing pole stuck into the ground beside him.

"Look!" Patricia exclaimed. "His frying pan is back!"

Keeley looked. The pan, worn from years of rough use, was sitting by the firepit in its usual place. Keeley remembered seeing the bundle in her teacher's arms. "Let's wake him up and ask him where he found it."

"No, I have a better idea." Patricia picked a bouquet of wildflowers, tied the stems together with some long grass, and put it gently down on the old trapper's chest.

"That doesn't give us any information," Keeley protested as they walked away.

"No," said Patricia, "but when he wakes up he'll think he has a girlfriend." They laughed as they ran into town.

Patricia was also the one who suggested they get permission to take Dexter for a walk. He was the scruffy little white terrier that lived next to the stables. "We can walk up and down the streets with a dog, and no one will wonder what we're up to."

It was a good suggestion. Dexter generally roamed the town quite freely, but Keeley liked holding onto his leash as he pranced along beside them. She felt like one of the rich, grand ladies of Lethbridge, where she used to live. The only problem was, Dexter wanted to stop every few feet to sniff at something, so the girls didn't move along as quickly as Keeley wanted to. Still, it was fun being with the dog.

They walked up and down Dominion Street, then along the back streets, then back to Dominion. There was no sign of Miss Griffin.

"Let's check the saloon," Patricia suggested.

"Miss Griffin won't be in there."

"No, but the army officer she talked to at the ceremony might be. Maybe he'll know where she is."

"Why would he know?"

"Maybe he secretly loves her," Patricia said, "but he can't marry her because he has pledged to the King never to marry until the British Empire rules the whole world. He loves her very much, and he wears his heart on his sleeve. Miss Griffin is stealing things in hopes of building a secret hideaway where they can be together and the King can't find them …"

"Did you say his heart is on his sleeve?" Keeley asked. "Patricia, you read *too many* books!"

Since they had no other ideas, they went to the saloon.

They stood on an upturned soapbox and looked in the window. The saloon was crowded. Some men were standing at the bar, some were snoring under a back table, and others, including women, were at the gambling tables.

"Do you see him?" Patricia asked.

"I don't think so," Keeley replied. "I wish the men at the bar would turn around."

"I saw someone thrown through the front window once," Patricia said. "That would make them turn around. But, unfortunately, that doesn't happen every day."

"Too bad," Keeley said. "They probably left already. She probably met him here earlier, and I missed them." Mr. Matheson had made her sit with her back to the window that morning. She had gotten more work done but hadn't had as much fun.

"This is pointless," Patricia said. "Come on, Dexter wants to keep walking." The small dog was straining on his leash. Keeley's arm kept flapping as Dexter tried to take off in different directions.

"Hey—do you hear that?"

They heard drumming sounds and a trumpet. It was faint at first, and then got suddenly louder as the parade turned onto the main street.

A large group of women marched down Dominion Street, their feet keeping time with the drum. The woman playing the trumpet looked as if she was having a great time.

The women carried signs that read "Down with the Demon Rum" and "Sign the Pledge." Sashes draped across their coats told everyone they were members of the Women's Christian Temperance Union.

The marchers filled the main street, drawing protests from the wagon-masters and cheers from children. The shoppers and the stopped traffic gave them an instant crowd as they came to a halt in front of the saloon. After a few final bangs on the drum, the music stopped, and one of the women stepped forward to give a speech.

"Ladies and gentlemen," she bellowed in a voice as big as her hat, "is there a greater example of the evils of alcohol than the vision of two innocent children standing at a saloon window, yearning for their father to stop drinking and return home?"

With a great swoop of her arm, she directed everyone's attention to Keeley and Patricia, standing on their soapbox in front of the saloon window.

The two girls stared at the crowd of faces that stared at them. Keeley hoped this wouldn't get back to her father.

"My father's not in there," Keeley started to say, but her voice was drowned out.

"We will now sing one of our special songs for these poor children," the march leader announced. The music started up again, and the marchers burst into song.

Keeley spotted Miss Griffin on the other side of the street, arms full of bundles again. "There she is!" she yelled to Patricia. In her excitement, Keeley let go of Dexter's leash. Dexter, who had been straining to chase a cat he'd spotted, leapt away from Keeley and ran straight into the group of marchers.

The women were so intent on their singing they didn't notice for a moment that a small dog had gotten lost in the forest of their skirts. Keeley thought Dexter must have nipped at an ankle, because the trumpet player suddenly hit a wrong note and began a great deal of hopping around.

Soon another marcher was hopping and grabbing her ankle. The singing turned to yells.

"What's going on out here?" The saloonkeeper stormed outside. He spied Keeley and Patricia, still standing at the window. "You two again! I've told you to stay away from here. It's bad for business to have two children staring through the window at the customers. This time, I'm going to tell your parents!"

He reached out to grab Keeley. Patricia threw herself at him, pushing Keeley out of the way.

"Run!" she yelled.

Keeley ran. Miss Griffin was already quite far down the street. The marchers were now completely tangled together, mixed up with their banners and the leash of a small, yapping dog. Keeley ran around them.

Miss Griffin left the main street, turning down where she had gone the week before. Keeley, breathing hard, held back a little so she wouldn't be spotted.

Miss Griffin walked quickly through the clearing and past one of the tent camps, where some of the miners were living temporarily. She didn't look back once.

Keeley followed her all the way to the edge of the forest. Just then, she heard a bark.

Dexter had followed her.

"Go back!" Keeley hissed at him, waving her arms. "Go home!"

Dexter, thinking she was playing a game, barked again and danced about on his hind legs. Keeley could see that he'd lost his leash.

Keeley found a stick, waved it in the air to get Dexter's attention, then threw it as far as she could. Dexter took off after it. Keeley hesitated just long enough to see the stick land in a pail of water being used by one of the campers to wash his socks. The water splashed up into his face.

The marchers were now
completely tangled together,
mixed up with their
banners and the leash
of a small, yapping dog.

As the camper groped for something to wipe the soapy water out of his eyes, Keeley spun around and plunged into the thick pine forest after her teacher.

CHAPTER Nº 8

The trees folded around Keeley as she ran down the narrow path, straining her eyes for a glimpse of Miss Griffin. Having to turn Dexter away had allowed Miss Griffin to get farther ahead of her.

The pathway was straight and clear at first, then it became bendy, heading this way, then that. It went up little hills and down into little valleys. Except for going up and down, there was little difference for Keeley between the hills and valleys. In either place, all she could see were trees.

Then she came to a spot where the pathway split into two. She stood at the fork in the path, wondering which way to go.

Keeley listened hard, trying to hear Miss Griffin's footfalls on the ground, but all she heard was the whistle of air moving through the pines, the singing of the birds, and the scurrying of animals that Keeley hoped were ground squirrels and not bears.

Lines from a poem she'd had to learn in school, as part of a detention, came into her head:

I'll walk where my own nature would be leading;
It vexes me to choose another guide;
Where the grey flocks in ferny glens are feeding;
Where the wild wind blows on the mountain side.

Keeley looked at the two pathways. Down which one would her nature lead her?

"Emily Brontë probably wasn't chasing her teacher through the forest when she wrote that," Keeley muttered. The poem didn't help her at all.

Still, if Emily Brontë became a famous poet that way, maybe it will make me a famous something, too. Keeley decided her nature was leading her to take the path on the left. She hoped it would make her famous as a reporter, not as a bear's dinner.

This path also split in two, then it split again. Sometimes it seemed to disappear completely or lead directly into a thicket of thorn bushes. And there was no sign of Miss Griffin.

It's getting dark, Keeley realized. She had thought that the dimming light was because of all the trees, but looking up at the sky, she knew that the sun had gone down.

Maybe I'd better get back, she thought. She turned around and started to retrace her steps.

The trees looked different on her way back, or maybe they all looked the same. She couldn't tell whether she was going the way she had come or not.

The darkness was coming faster now. It changed the shapes of the trees into shadows and monsters, and the wind made the monsters bend to grab at her.

"They're only trees," Keeley told herself, trying to keep herself calm. It almost worked. Then a loud noise sent her running.

Fears of bears and monsters pushed her to keep running, even as tree branches whipped at her face and snagged at her clothes. She ran smack into tree trunks and had no idea whether she was still on the path, but she kept going.

Until she tripped on a tree root and landed face down in the dirt.

Pain shot through her ankle.

This was not a moment to be quiet and brave. This was a time to yell and cry, and Keeley did plenty of both things, even calling out for Miss Griffin. By the time her throat was sore from yelling and she was tired out from crying, night had truly arrived.

Keeley tried to get to her feet, but her ankle hurt too much. The pain was like fire, even though the rest of her was getting cold.

There was nothing to do but wait until daylight. People would know she was missing, and they'd come looking for her. At least, she hoped they would. If not, maybe she'd turn into one of those wild creatures Patricia had talked about. She'd grow lots of hair and would run around late at night, stealing chickens and frying pans.

Keeley wondered whether her teacher was also lost. It was hard to imagine Miss Griffin not being absolutely sure of herself all the time.

She felt the ground around her, inch by inch, to see what was there. It was a little like being trapped in the mine. She'd gotten through that night; she'd get through this one. She lay down and tried to get comfortable. If only her ankle didn't hurt so much. If only the wind would stop making scary noises in the trees. If only she weren't so cold.

She heard something shuffling in the underbrush and sat bolt upright again. Whatever it was, it was coming closer. Keeley's heart beat faster and faster. She was too scared to scream, and then it was there!

It leapt onto her lap and licked her face.

"Dexter!" Keeley wrapped her arms around the squirming, happy little dog. "How did you find me?"

Dexter was warm and furry, and very brave for such a little dog. He sniffed at Keeley, gave her sore ankle a few kisses, then curled up in her arms.

All through the dark night, Dexter protected Keeley, and Keeley protected Dexter. They both slept soundly on the soft forest floor.

First, there was a growl, then there was a bark, and then there was a little stub of a tail wagging in her face. Keeley was now wide awake.

A girl around Keeley's age was standing among the trees just a few feet away. Her dark braids were longer than Keeley's. The dress she wore was simpler than the ones worn by most of the town girls, but the string of beads around her neck made it look very pretty.

Dexter growled, took two steps toward the girl, then two steps back, until the girl went down on her knees. Dexter accepted her invitation to introduce himself, and within moments he was jumping on her and licking her face.

"My name is Keeley," Keeley said, although the girl was clearly more interested in the dog than in her. "Can you help me? I've hurt my ankle."

The girl kept playing with Dexter.

Keeley spoke again. "My father's probably very worried. I spent the night here, but I wasn't supposed to. I was following my teacher, and I tripped and, well, here I am." Keeley wondered whether she should mention getting lost but decided she didn't need to share everything. It would make her feel foolish, since this other girl looked as if she knew her way around the forest.

But the other girl continued to ignore her. She gave no clue that she even realized that Keeley was talking. Keeley got annoyed. Sure, Dexter was a cute dog, but he wasn't *that* cute!

"My ankle is hurting a lot," Keeley said. "Stop playing with the stupid dog and go get help!"

The girl didn't even look up.

"Hey—I'm talking to you!" Keeley tossed a handful of pine needles at the girl. The girl looked up at her, reluctantly stopped playing with Dexter, got to her feet, and slipped away into the woods.

"She's so rude," Keeley fumed at the dog.

Dexter obviously didn't mind that. He took one look at the frown on Keeley's face, then trotted away after the girl with the long, dark braids.

Keeley tried again to stand up, but the pain in her ankle made it impossible. She sat on the ground, grumbling, and thought about what to do if the girl didn't bring anyone back. She looked around for a long stick she could use as a crutch. She'd still be lost but at least she'd be moving.

She spied a suitable stick, but it was too far away to grab from where she was sitting. She inched toward it on her backside.

When she reached the stick, she saw it was quite rotten. She spotted another a greater distance away. To get to it, she had to flatten herself on her belly and crawl under a low tree branch. Her ankle didn't like the change, but she could move a lot faster.

She pulled herself along, hands first, grabbing at rocks and roots and the pine-covered ground. Her hand cupped around something that wasn't a rock or a root. Keeley looked up and gave a cry of surprise. She was holding onto the moccasin-covered foot of a man. He had long, dark braids, too, like the girl beside him. Dexter was with them.

"You're a strange-looking snake," the man said, smiling.

"I'm not a snake," Keeley replied. "I'm a girl, and I've hurt my ankle."

"Come with me, girl who is not a snake." He bent down and put his arms around her.

"But I don't know you," Keeley said. "Where are you taking me?"

He scooped her up. "My name is Walter Two Moons, and I am taking you to meet my family.

Aren't you hungry?" They headed off through the forest.

The day was just beginning. Wisps of fog played along the branches, and the sunlight through it made the spiderwebs glow like magic. Walter Two Moons had no trouble finding the trails, and they made their way through the trees without being hit by branches.

"I'm so glad you found me," Keeley said. "I was chasing my teacher, and I got lost."

"Were you playing a game?"

"No, I was …," Keeley was about to say she was being a reporter, but she didn't think real reporters like Cora Hind ever got lost in the woods. "Yes, it was a game, but I guess it wasn't a very good game."

"It's lucky that Makskii, my daughter, was out looking for herbs," he said.

"Yes, it is lucky," Keeley agreed. "Thank you for helping me," she said to the girl. The girl didn't reply.

"I hate to say this about another girl," Keeley

said, "but your daughter is awfully rude. I talk to her, and she ignores me. Maybe she doesn't like me."

"She hears with her heart, not her ears. Speak to her with your heart, and she'll hear you."

Keeley was glad to know that the girl didn't dislike her and wondered how to talk with her heart. "I'm used to talking with words," she said. She went on to say that she lived in Frank. "Do you know where that is?"

"That's the town they built in the way of the mountain," Walter Two Moons said.

"You mean, in the valley of the mountain."

"No, in the way of the mountain. When the mountain decides to get up and walk, the town will be in its way."

"I've heard that story," Keeley said, "but it's just a story, isn't it, like 'Jack and the Beanstalk'?"

Keeley kept talking and talking until Walter Two Moons said, "You are just like the little dog. You both make big noises for such small creatures."

Keeley shut up. When she did, she was able to hear the sounds of the forest in the morning. It was quiet and noisy at the same time. She saw a family of deer through the trees, standing and watching as the humans passed by.

The trees opened up to a small meadow. Sun burning through the mist gave the whole clearing a soft, yellow glow.

Three tipis rose up in the meadow like trees. Women with long braids and beaded belts around their full-skirted dresses looked up from their tasks. Children ran to greet Walter Two Moons, his daughter, and Keeley. The children got close, then they hung back, shy in front of this strange girl.

Keeley looked at the people, and the people looked at her, as Walter Two Moons carried her into the camp.

Keeley was put down gently on a log by the cook fire. The men talked with the women in a language Keeley didn't understand.

"I tripped," Keeley said. "And I got lost." She was a little nervous among these new people.

She wasn't sure whether they understood her, so she smiled. At least they could understand her face.

Keeley's foot was eased out of its shoe and stocking. It was bigger than her foot should be and very sore.

One of the women packed some wet leaves around it and wrapped it up with a cloth. Another of the women took off her shawl and wrapped it around Keeley's shoulders. A tin mug of hot tea was put into Keeley's hands.

Before she could take a sip of tea, she had another surprise.

Miss Griffin stepped out of one of the tipis.

Keeley stared at her teacher, and her teacher stared back. Into their staring match walked a man with a long brown beard. He was carrying an armload of firewood.

"Keeley," Miss Griffin said, "I'd like you to meet Fred. Fred is my brother."

CHAPTER No 10

Clearly, neither Miss Griffin nor her brother was happy to see Keeley. Fred crouched down to stack the wood by the firepit, then rose up again and glared at her.

Keeley didn't glare back, but she did *stare* back. Fred Griffin's beard took up most of his face, but she could see that he and her teacher shared the same nose, forehead, and eyes. In fact, he looked exactly the way Miss Griffin would look if she had a beard.

"You look alike," Keeley said.

"We're twins," Miss Griffin replied. "What are

Clearly, neither Miss Griffin
nor her brother was
happy to see Keeley.

you doing here, Keeley?" She used her annoyed teacher voice.

Keeley wilted a little then. "Having a cup of tea?"

"I asked what you are doing here."

"I was following you," Keeley answered. There was no point in trying to hide the truth from Miss Griffin. "I got held up by Dexter, then I got lost, then I hurt my foot."

"Now the whole town will be up here," Fred said.

"She doesn't know where she is," Walter Two Moons said. "How can she lead others here?"

"Her family will be swarming all over here, looking for her."

"There's just my father," Keeley began.

"A most reasonable man," Miss Griffin said. "Calm down, Fred. Keeley, why were you following me?" Miss Griffin and her brother sat down near Keeley.

"I was being a reporter," Keeley said, looking at the ground. It sounded foolish now. "I was trying to solve a mystery."

"What mystery?" Miss Griffin asked. "No, don't tell me. I can guess. Things have been disappearing all over town." She frowned at her brother.

"I was trying to catch the thief," Keeley said.

"I couldn't think of another way to manage," Fred said sadly. "I've only just met these good people." He waved his arm at the people around the fire. "I had to survive and I didn't know who to trust. I just borrowed those things. I was planning on returning them."

"When you borrow something without the owner's permission, of course you will be mistaken for a thief," Miss Griffin snapped at her brother. It sounded to Keeley as if they'd had this argument before. To Keeley she said, "I've replaced things as I was able to do on a teacher's salary. Nearly everything has already been returned to the owners."

"Except for Mrs. Nesbit's pie, of course," said Keeley.

"It wasn't very good," Fred said. Miss Griffin frowned at him again, but Keeley smiled. She'd had Mrs. Nesbit's pie before. It *wasn't* very good.

"Why are you hiding out?" Keeley asked Fred. "Why don't you stay in Frank? The boarding house is nice. That's where I live." She looked around her at the camp. "Although this is awfully nice, too," she said and smiled at the people around the fire. They smiled back. Maybe she could come back here and stay with them sometime.

"Don't tell her anything," Fred said. "She'll spread the news everywhere."

"She would be more likely to talk if she doesn't understand," Walter Two Moons said. "Children are usually wise about these things."

Keeley liked the sound of that.

"She'll turn me in for a penny's worth of candy," Fred insisted.

"Stop being so unpleasant," Miss Griffin said. "There are a lot more good people in the world than bad ones." She moved over to sit beside Keeley. "My brother is a deserter from the army."

"She won't understand," Fred started.

"Stop!" Miss Griffin said to him. "Keeley has been a frequent trial to me, but she is smart.

She'll understand." She turned back to Keeley. "You know that Canada is now involved in a war in South Africa."

"The Boer War," Keeley said, then spelled out the word *Boer*. "I know it's a war and that we're fighting because England is fighting, and we're supposed to do what the King tells us to do, but I don't really know why."

"The British are fighting Dutch settlers—called the Boers—and the native Africans for control of the country," Miss Griffin said. "Canada is fighting on the side of the British. My brother was a soldier in that war, but he didn't want to fight. He left his unit without permission, which is a serious crime in the army. He made his way back to Canada on a trading ship. A short while ago, I found out he was here." Miss Griffin smiled. "Andy Grissick tracked down his frying pan and told me where to find Fred."

That solved the mystery of the frying pan. "Why did your brother come here?"

"He knew I lived here. Our parents died when we were younger. We only have each other."

That was a lot of information. Keeley took a swallow of her tea. It warmed her insides. Her foot was feeling better, too. It wasn't throbbing nearly so badly.

"Why didn't you want to fight?" she asked Fred. "I think it would be exciting."

"I thought it would be, too," he said. "That's why I joined up. I knew it would be dangerous, and I knew I'd probably have to kill people. It's not a nice thing to do, but I didn't think about it much—if someone was going to shoot at me, then, of course, I was going to shoot back."

He picked up the pot of tea and tried to pour some in a cup, but his hands were shaking too much with emotion. Miss Griffin took the pot from him and poured him something to drink. She filled the other mugs, as well.

Fred took a deep drink of tea, then continued. "The fighting was bad enough, but I stood my ground. I did my duty to the King, and to the

Queen before him, although exactly why they required me to kill those people, I'll never understand. But then they turned me into a jailer. Boers and black Africans were rounded up and put into separate concentration camps. While my brothers-in-arms burned down farms, I watched Boer women and children die of pneumonia, starvation, and dysentery. But those camps were palaces compared to the camps for black Africans."

He tossed the remains of the tea into the fire.

"What kind of courage does it take to keep children locked up? Where is the honour in that? I complained to my officers. They told me to shut up and do my job. I complained to my friends. They laughed. They weren't my friends any more. I didn't know them. So, I left. For a while, I borrowed—stole—to get by. Now I live with civilized people."

He stopped talking then. Keeley was glad he had stopped. Her head was spinning. None of the speechmakers on Empire Day had talked about this. The day wasn't quite so sunny now.

Miss Griffin spoke quietly. "If my brother is found, he'll be arrested. He'll probably be shot. That is the usual punishment for desertion."

"So—what's your decision?" Fred asked in a quiet voice.

Keeley didn't understand. "My decision?"

"When you go home, are you going to tell the constable that you saw me?" Fred hesitated a moment, then added, "The army may offer a reward for such information."

Keeley was surprised to realize that the word *reward* had no effect on her.

Miss Griffin reached over and laid her hand gently on Keeley's arm. "This is a grown-up decision, Keeley. There are consequences, real consequences, to whatever you choose. You have duties as a friend and duties as a citizen, and sometimes those duties conflict with each other. That's when you have to make a choice. And you have to choose, and soon, because we have to get you back to your father."

"How do I decide?" Keeley asked.

"That's a good question and a wise question," Walter Two Moons said. "Ask yourself what is most important to you. When you know that, you'll know what to do."

The grown-ups left Keeley alone for a little while. She was surprised to hear Miss Griffin and Fred speak the same language as the others. A different language is something that can be learned, she realized. *I could learn it.*

Makskii sat down on the log beside Keeley. She had two dolls in her hand, made from wood and deerskin. She gave one to Keeley. Makskii smiled as they played together. Keeley felt her heart speak to Makskii and heard Makskii's heart speak to her. It was easier than she'd imagined.

As Keeley played, she thought about how much she missed her mother and how alone she'd feel if she lost her father, too. Miss Griffin probably felt the same way. She was a teacher, but she probably had feelings the way normal people did. She would be very sad if she lost her brother.

However, Keeley was also a citizen of Canada, even though she was just a child. She had a duty to obey the law and to support the Empire. But what if she didn't agree with what the Empire was doing? Could a child disagree with a King?

Keeley played with Makskii, ate dried bear meat and berries with the others around the fire, and watched Miss Griffin be with her brother. When the time came to go home, Keeley knew what she was going to do.

CHAPTER No. 11

Keeley sat on her window-seat bed, looking out at Turtle Mountain. She loved watching it change colour, from dark grey to black, as the evening slipped into night. Her ankle felt a lot better. It was only sprained and would be completely fine soon.

It had been quite a day. There was a lot to think about.

"You seem destined to have adventures," her father told Keeley after Walter Two Moons had carried her up the steps of the boarding house. "Which means that I am destined to go grey at a young age."

"You will look very handsome with grey hair," Violet said. She had worked with some of the other women to prepare lunches for the search party that had been called back from the forest when Keeley reappeared.

"Don't you know better than to go running off into the forest?" one of the searchers asked her. "It's not a safe place for a little girl."

Keeley remembered how well she'd slept on the pine needles and how beautiful the forest had looked in the morning. She'd spend more nights there on her own, if she could figure out how to do it without worrying people.

"What were you doing there, anyway?" someone else asked.

"I was running after Dexter," she replied. It was only a small lie.

"From now on, let Dexter look after himself. Dogs are a whole lot smarter than little girls," one man said.

And I'm a whole lot smarter than you, Keeley

thought. She was certainly smart enough not to say so out loud.

Before leaving the camp, she had worked out a plan with Miss Griffin to make a pie to sneak onto Mrs. Nesbit's windowsill. She hoped she'd be able to hide and see Mrs. Nesbit's reaction.

"You weren't just chasing Dexter, were you?" her father asked as he said goodnight. "There's more to the story than you're telling me, isn't there?"

Keeley nodded.

"Can you tell me?"

"I promised not to." It was a shame, though, thought Keeley. Her adventure would have made a great newspaper story.

"I wouldn't want you to break your promise." He kissed her goodnight.

"Pop?" Keeley asked. "If you had to choose between your friend and your king, who would you choose?"

"My friend," her father answered without hesitation. "Kings come and go, but friends are forever."

"Then I made the right choice," Keeley said. "Pop, the world isn't just one way, is it?"

"What do you mean?"

The thought in Keeley's head was almost too big for her brain. She struggled to understand it and put it into words. "The world isn't just one way," she said again. "It's different ways, because everyone sees it differently."

Her father nodded. He could see there was more she had to say, so he waited for it.

"And the world can change, too. People can decide something and change things. They can make things happen."

"You've discovered the secret to happiness," her father said. "Goodnight, my smart girl."

Keeley smiled in the dark at her newfound sense of power. She was no longer just a child. She was a girl who had made a grown-up decision.

Miss Griffin was no longer just a teacher. She was a woman who loved her brother and had a whole range of feelings and abilities, beyond her ability to hand out detentions.

The forest wasn't just a dark, green place full of dangers. It was a place of comforts and wonders, dangers, too, but also a place that was home to many creatures and people, including a girl who listened with her heart.

The world hadn't changed, but the way Keeley saw it was very different. It felt good, but it was a little scary, too.

Keeley looked out the window at the night gathering around the mountain. "At least there is only one way to see a mountain," she said, "strong, solid, and the same, forever and ever."

She kept looking out the window until it was too dark to see anything, then she curled up under her blankets and went to sleep.

Dear Reader,

Welcome back to the continuing adventures of Our Canadian Girl! It's been another exciting year for us here at Penguin, publishing new stories and continuing the adventures of twelve terrific girls. The best part of this past year, though, has been the wonderful letters we've received from readers like you, telling us about your favourite Our Canadian Girl story, and the parts you liked the most. Best of all, you told us which stories you would like to read, and we were amazed! There are so many remarkable stories in Canadian history. It seems that wherever we live, great stories live too, in our towns and cities, on our rivers and mountains. Thank you so much for sharing them.

So please, stay in touch. Write letters, log on to our website (www.ourcanadiangirl.ca), let us know what you think of Our Canadian Girl. We're listening.

Sincerely,
Barbara Berson

Canada's

1608 Samuel de Champlain establishes the first fortified trading post at Quebec.

1755 The British expel the entire French population of Acadia (today's Maritime provinces), sending them into exile.

1759 The British defeat the French in the Battle of the Plains of Abraham.

1776 The 13 Colonies revolt against Britain, and the Loyalists flee to Canada.

1784 Rachel

1812 The United States declares war against Canada.

1837 Calling for responsible government, the Patriotes, following Louis-Joseph Papineau, rebel in Lower Canada; William Lyon Mackenzie leads the uprising in Upper Canada.

1845 The expedition of Sir John Franklin to the Arctic ends when the ship is frozen in the pack ice; the fate of its crew remains a mystery.

1867 New Brunswick, Nova Scotia and the United Province of Canada come together in Confederation to form the Dominion of Canada.

1869 Louis Riel leads his Métis followers in the Red River Rebellion.

1870 Manitoba joins Canada. The Northwest Territories become an official territory of Canada.

1871 British Columbia joins Canada.

Timeline

1873
Prince Edward Island joins Canada.

1885
At Craigellachie, British Columbia, the last spike is driven to complete the building of the Canadian Pacific Railway.

1896
Gold is discovered on Bonanza Creek, a tributary of the Klondike River.

1898
The Yukon Territory becomes an official territory of Canada.

1905
Alberta and Saskatchewan join Canada.

1914
Britain declares war on Germany, and Canada, because of its ties to Britain, is at war too.

1917
In the Halifax harbour, two ships collide, causing an explosion that leaves more than 1,600 dead and 9,000 injured.

1918
As a result of the Wartime Elections Act, the women of Canada are given the right to vote in federal elections.

1939
Canada declares war on Germany seven days after war is declared by Britain and France.

1945
World War II ends conclusively with the dropping of atomic bombs on Hiroshima and Nagasaki.

1949
Newfoundland, under the leadership of Joey Smallwood, joins Canada.

1885
Marie-Claire

1902
Keeley

1914
Millie

Keeley is a daring girl living in Frank, Alberta.
Be sure to join Keeley and the colourful
characters of Frank on their first adventure.
The Girl from Turtle Mountain is in stores now.

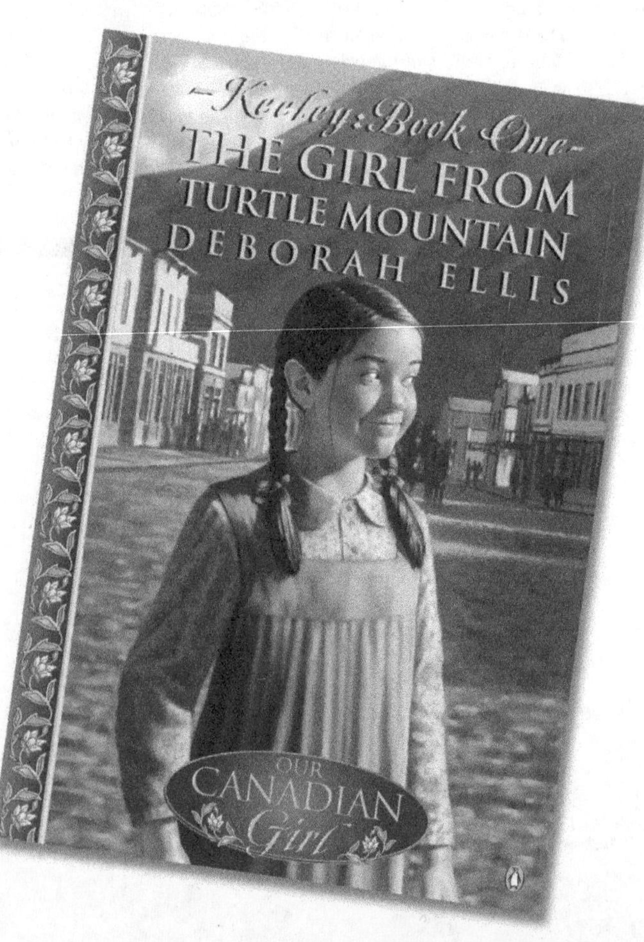

Don't miss a single Keeley adventure!
Book Three will be available Fall 2006

Meet all the Our Canadian Girls!

Learn more about these strong, smart, and courageous girls by visiting **www.ourcanadiangirl.ca**

OUR CANADIAN Girl

Keeley: Book Two

KEELEY'S BIG STORY

DEBORAH ELLIS